CAMILLA CAN VOTE

Celebrating the Centennial of Women's Right to Vote

By **Mary Morgan Ketchel**

with Senator Marsha Blackburn

Forefront
BOOKS

Published in Nashville, Tennessee.

Published by Forefront Books.
Design and Illustration by Bill Kersey, KerseyGraphics

ISBN: 978-1-948677-54-7
ISBN: 978-1-948677-55-4 (ebook)

Printed in the United States of America

20 21 22 23 24   10 9 8 7 6 5 4 3 2 1

VOTES FOR WOMEN

Camilla had been waiting for this day for weeks! Her class was finally on their field trip to the history museum, and she was so excited! History was her favorite!

"Votes for Women!" Camilla read the words on the sign above the entrance.

"Class!" Ms. Travis called to get everyone's attention. "Who has heard of the Women's Suffrage Movement?"

A few students raised their hands. Others shook their heads.

"Suffrage?" Camilla wondered aloud. "Sounds a little scary."

Ms. Travis smiled and replied, "Actually, the Women's Suffrage Movement refers to a very brave group of women who did something really BIG! Are you ready to go inside and learn more?"

"YES!" the entire class shouted in unison.

As the students filed into the museum, a docent—
a fancy name for a tour guide—met them in the
lobby. Her name was Wendy.

"Welcome, everyone!" Wendy said excitedly. "I am so happy you are here today. I can't wait to show you our Women's Suffrage exhibit! By the time you leave today, you will have learned so much about this period in our nation's history that you'll feel like you've traveled back in time."

Camilla's class followed Wendy through the large doors to the exhibit room—a huge room full of glass cases with mannequins dressed in old-timey clothes, huge black and white photos, and other old items inside. At each station, a sign told the story of that piece of history.

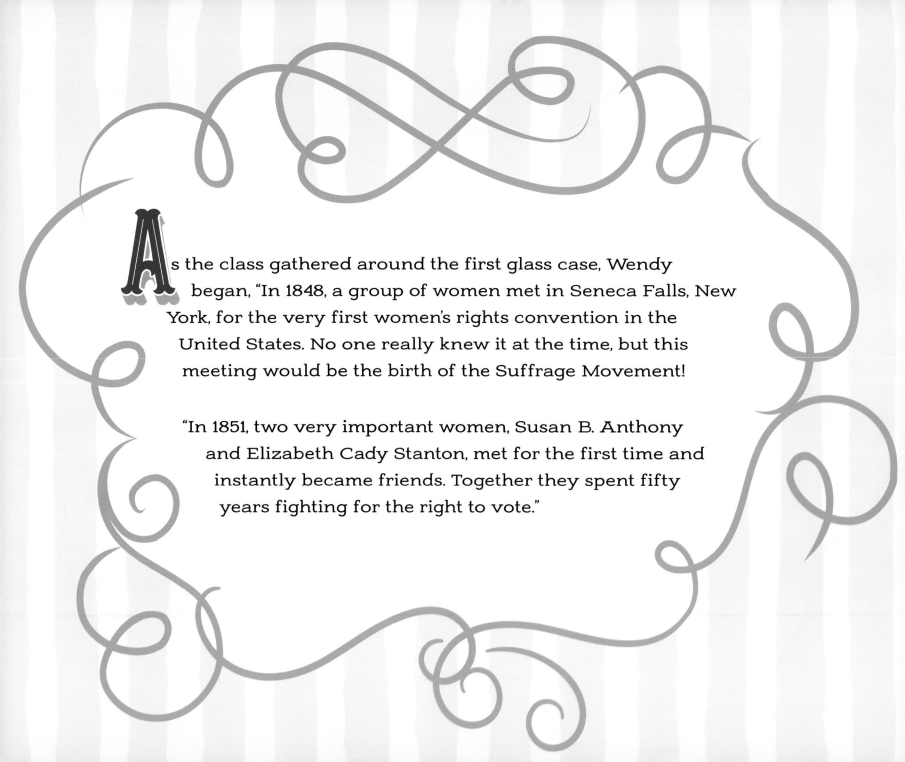

As the class gathered around the first glass case, Wendy began, "In 1848, a group of women met in Seneca Falls, New York, for the very first women's rights convention in the United States. No one really knew it at the time, but this meeting would be the birth of the Suffrage Movement!

"In 1851, two very important women, Susan B. Anthony and Elizabeth Cady Stanton, met for the first time and instantly became friends. Together they spent fifty years fighting for the right to vote."

"It's hard to imagine now, but women like your mother and Ms. Travis could not vote then. Only men voted," Wendy explained.

That's weird, Camilla thought.

"More women were learning about Miss Anthony and Miss Stanton and the fight for the right to vote. Mothers, grandmothers, daughters, and friends were joining in the fight," Wendy continued.

"Younger women like Carrie Chapman Catt and Anna Howard Shaw started to lead the movement. And with each decade, more women joined the effort.

"A lady named Alice Paul started to organize 'Votes for Women' protests across the country. They even picketed the White House and President Woodrow Wilson to support their right to vote. Many of the women held signs that read, 'Mr. President, how long must women wait for liberty?'"

"Then came the turning point for votes for women. On August 18, 1920, in Nashville, Tennessee, the state legislature would decide to either ratify (to vote for) or nullify (to vote against) the 19th Amendment. Pro-suffrage and anti-suffrage groups set up headquarters in the Hermitage Hotel to talk to the legislators and the governor.

"There, the pro-suffragists (or 'Suffs') passed out yellow roses for the supporters to wear. Meanwhile, the anti-Suffragists (or 'Antis') wore red roses. People called it 'The War of the Roses.'

"With yellow roses pinned to their dresses, the Suffs were ready to march to the capitol building for the historic vote. If Tennessee voted in favor of the 19th Amendment, women across the United States would be granted the right to vote!"

"And now we come to a special part of our tour!" Wendy said to the class.

"I am going to give each of you a yellow rose pin, the symbol of the Women's Suffrage Movement."

Camilla's eyes grew wide with excitement! And her classmates squealed as they each got their yellow rose pin.

When it was Camilla's turn, Wendy stuck a pin onto Camilla's blouse. But then something happened! Just as Camilla touched the pin, the rose was no longer a pin at all! Instead, it transformed into a real yellow rose!

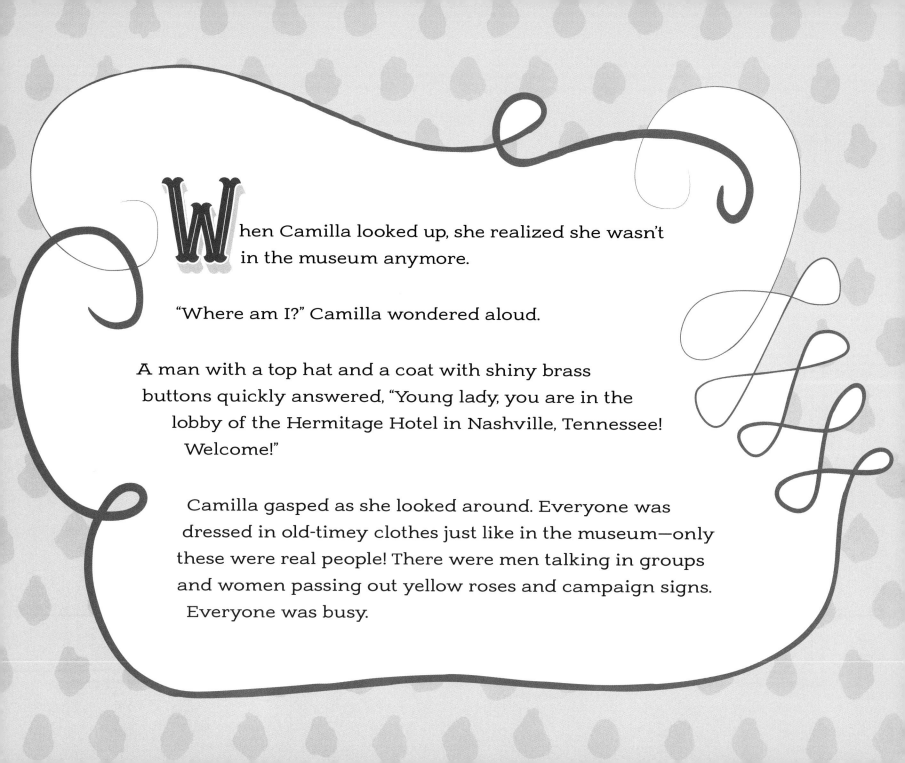

When Camilla looked up, she realized she wasn't in the museum anymore.

"Where am I?" Camilla wondered aloud.

A man with a top hat and a coat with shiny brass buttons quickly answered, "Young lady, you are in the lobby of the Hermitage Hotel in Nashville, Tennessee! Welcome!"

Camilla gasped as she looked around. Everyone was dressed in old-timey clothes just like in the museum—only these were real people! There were men talking in groups and women passing out yellow roses and campaign signs. Everyone was busy.

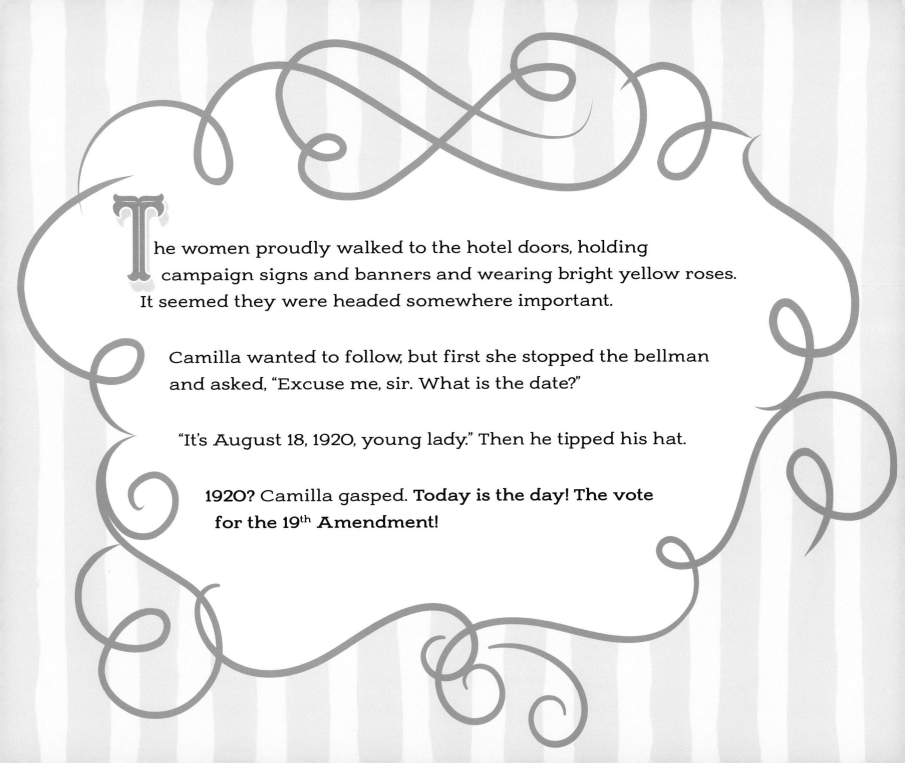

The women proudly walked to the hotel doors, holding campaign signs and banners and wearing bright yellow roses. It seemed they were headed somewhere important.

Camilla wanted to follow, but first she stopped the bellman and asked, "Excuse me, sir. What is the date?"

"It's August 18, 1920, young lady." Then he tipped his hat.

1920? Camilla gasped. **Today is the day! The vote for the 19th Amendment!**

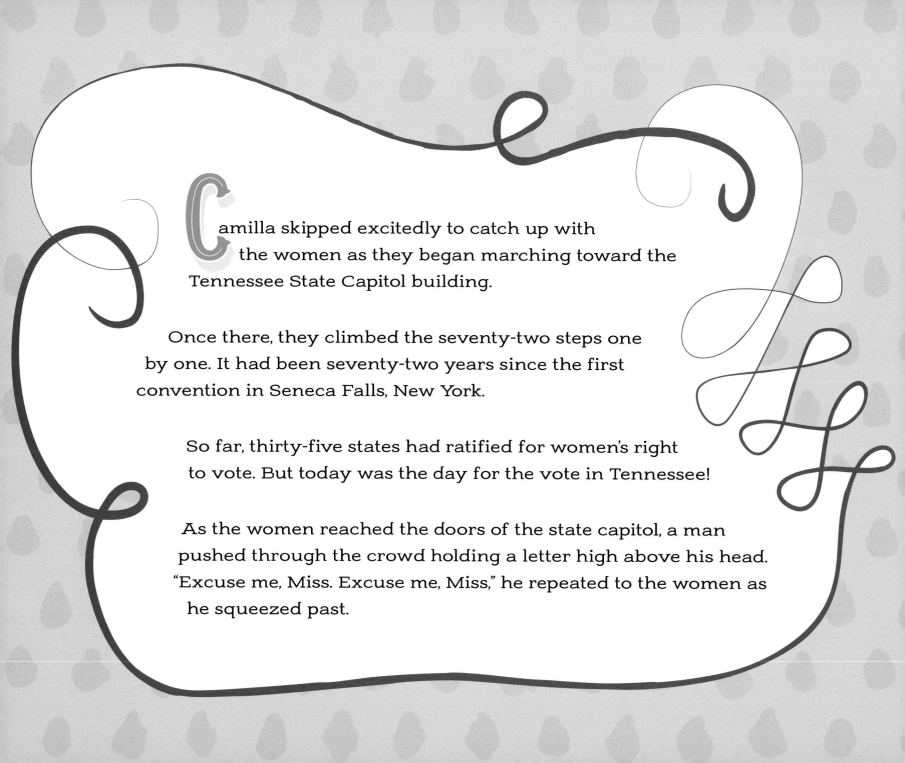

Camilla skipped excitedly to catch up with the women as they began marching toward the Tennessee State Capitol building.

Once there, they climbed the seventy-two steps one by one. It had been seventy-two years since the first convention in Seneca Falls, New York.

So far, thirty-five states had ratified for women's right to vote. But today was the day for the vote in Tennessee!

As the women reached the doors of the state capitol, a man pushed through the crowd holding a letter high above his head. "Excuse me, Miss. Excuse me, Miss," he repeated to the women as he squeezed past.

"That's Representative Harry T. Burn. He's against the vote." Camilla heard one woman say to another.

"What is he holding?" several women asked.

"It looks like a letter," said another.

The letter was from his suffragist mother, Miss Febb, asking him to change his mind and vote "aye" for votes for women.

Dear Son,

Hurrah, and vote for Suffrage! Don't keep them in doubt. I noticed Chandler's speech. It was very bitter.

I've been watching to see how you stood but have not seen anything yet.

Don't forget to be a good boy and help Mrs. Catt with her "rats." Is she the one that put "rat" in "ratification"?

No more from Mama this time.

With lots of love,

Mama

Back at the capitol, the suffragists made their way into the House chamber and stood in the gallery where they could see what was happening on the House floor. Everyone watched in anticipation.

Both sides—the representatives who supported the "Suffs" and those for the "Antis"—gave speeches.

The House Speaker addressed the legislators, "The hour has come. The battle has been fought and won, and I move . . . that the motion to concur in the Senate action goes where it belongs—to the table."

He wanted to delay the vote! But his plan failed and that meant the vote would still happen. The only thing left to do was vote.

The House clerk began calling roll and with each name called, the men would cast their vote with a "nay" for no and an "aye" for yes.

Everyone listened intently. When the clerk called Harry T. Burn's name, to everyone's surprise, he answered, "Aye!"

The chamber erupted with shouts and cheers. With this one vote, the 19th Amendment became law. Women now had the right to vote!

As Harry T. Burn left the hall, everyone cheered, "Hooray! Today is the day!"

"Hooray!" Camilla joined in the celebration.

"Inside voice, Camilla," Ms. Travis said to Camilla.

Camilla looked down and touched her pin—no longer a real yellow rose.

"How? . . . But I was just in . . ." Camilla started to explain but wasn't sure she could.

She followed Ms. Travis and the rest of the class to the art room.

After the class had finished their artwork, Ms. Travis said, "All right, class. Our trip through history must end."

Camilla took a deep breath. She couldn't believe what had happened today. It had felt so real—like she was actually there!

Then she thought to herself, **Yes! This was an AMAZING trip!**

On the bus ride back to school, Camilla thought about all she learned.

She couldn't imagine a world where grown-up women like her mother, Ms. Travis, or Wendy didn't have the right to vote. But women spent seventy-two years fighting, petitioning, and educating just to have their voice heard.

She was so grateful for the work of those brave, dedicated, and determined women!